THE Truth About BIGFOOT

by Tracy Sue Walker

illustrated by Chris Jevons

SCHOLASTIC INC.

ISBN 978-1-338-61750-4

10 9 8 7 6 5 4 3 2 1   20 21 22 23 24

Printed in the U.S.A.   40
First printing 2020

Book design by Jennifer Rinaldi

CHAPTER ONE
FRISNER'S PRISONERS

HERE'S THE DEAL. THERE ARE LOTS OF MAGICAL powers. Invisibility. Breathing fire. Flying. Having really big feet.

"What's magical about big feet?" you might think.

Exactly.

I'm Julian Fillmore, and my friends Ava Chen, Sarah Marco, and I are The Kids for Truth about Magical Creatures (KTMC for short). We're determined to prove that magical creatures aren't the greatest things since recess. Especially if your main claim to fame is needing an extra-large toenail clipper. Think I'm kidding?

You haven't met Bigfoot.

The worst thing in Mrs. Frisner's room is the dragon poster. It has a drawing of a blue dragon roasting a marshmallow with his fire-breath for a says at the bottom in big gold letters. Mrs. Frisner got it because she mailed in ten empty bags of Puffy Pals marshmallows.

Ava disagrees. She thinks the mermaid clock is awful. Her scaly green tail swings back and forth, back and forth. All. Day. Long. Plus, every hour on the hour, she announces in this squeaky giggle, "Have a FIN-tastic day!" followed by little bubble sounds.

Sarah, on the other hand, thinks the photo of the ogre should be the first thing to go. It hangs on the wall next to our classroom door. The ogre has beady blue eyes and a huge wart on his nose. "He gives me the creeps," she says. "It's like the painting of George Washington in my grandma's basement. His eyes follow you wherever you go."

Then there's the bulletin board. Mrs. Frisner's classroom is filled floor-to-ceiling with magical creatures, but the bulletin board is the centerpiece. It's at the back of the room, and the whole thing is covered with a map of the world. Mrs. Frisner makes little homemade flags taped to straight pins, and there are at least thirty of them. Each flag has the name of a magical creature written on it and where they're from. There's a troll flag stuck in Norway, a Sphinx flag in Egypt, different types of dragon flags stuck on all seven continents. You get the drift.

Everybody in our class, especially Mrs. Frisner, thinks magical creatures are the be all and end all, but not KTMC. We aren't fooled by Magicals. We know non-magical creatures—Ordinaries—deserve just as much attention. That's why we started KTMC and our blog, *Creature Feature*. We recently wrapped up our first investigation on unicorns, but there are so many Magicals out there, we've only scratched the surface.

Mrs. Frisner has a new Magical flag taped to a pin. She's rolling it between her thumb and index finger. "Next week we set out for our field trip," she says, rolling the flag the whole time. "Three days of science at Peaceful Pine State Park."

I glance across the room at Ava. She looks like she won the lottery. Some people love chocolate. Other people love sports. Ava loves science. She raises her hand.

Mrs. Frisner takes a deep breath. "Yes, Miss Chen?" she says. Her voice is low and sounds like my mom's minivan rolling down the gravel road behind our house.

"What kind of science? Biology?" Ava asks, sitting up in her desk.

"Possibly," Mrs. Frisner says, looking at the mermaid clock.

"Ecology?" Ava says.

Mrs. Frisner takes another deep breath. "Perhaps."

"Zoology?" Ava won't stop until she gets an answer.

Mrs. Frisner sighs, "Moving on, Ms. Chen."

Ava crosses her arms and slinks into her seat.

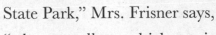

"While we're on the subject of Peaceful Pine State Park," Mrs. Frisner says, "who can tell me which magical creature has decided to make it his home?"

I look at Ava again. She catches my eye while scrawling something on her notebook, and when Mrs. Frisner turns her back, she holds it up. *Save Me!* it says, and I nod.

My friend Brandon Henderson raises his hand, and that's no surprise. He loves Magicals. Remember the unicorns I said we investigated? One of them is Brandon's.

"Mr. Henderson!" Mrs. Frisner points a stubby finger at him.

"Bigfoot?" he answers.

"Right you are!" Mrs. Frisner squeezes past our

desks so she can get to the bulletin board. Her skirt has little dragons all over it and it brushes the tops of her sandals when she walks. Her socks are covered in tiny unicorns. It's not a good combo.

"Mr. Henderson," she says, "you have the honor of placing our next flag!"

Brandon is at the bulletin board in three leaps.

"Right here on Peaceful Pine State Park!" Mrs. Frisner says, pointing at a spot on the map.

"Mrs. Frisner," Brandon says. "How do you know Bigfoot's really there? Nobody's gotten evidence."

Mrs. Frisner chuckles. Her laughter sounds like the motion-sensor witch my aunt Leslie puts on her front porch every Halloween. Every time someone walks past her, she waves her broom and says, "Trick or treat, smell my feet!" Then she cackles, "WaaHAHAHAHAheeheeheehee!" and ends with two coughs and a sputter.

"That's about to change, Mr. Henderson," Mrs. Frisner says. She opens her mouth to say more, but the last bell of the day rings. We bolt from our desks. Frisner's Prisoners are finally free.

CHAPTER 2
YOU'RE GETTING WARMER

"HOW CAN YOU FIND ANYTHING?" AVA ASKS, STARING into Sarah's locker.

"I have my own system," Sarah says as she crams her science book on the top shelf. "I know where everything is."

Ava shakes her head. "Scientists *can't* be messy. They need to be organized," she says.

"Yeah, well, I'm an artist. Messy is my mojo. Julian's a writer; he gets it," Sarah says, looking at me. "Ever seen his locker when he's working on a blog post?" Ava rolls her eyes.

There are notebooks in all sizes and colors shoved in Sarah's locker. She's our KTMC secretary, which means she keeps all our meeting and investigative notes. She flips through a purple notebook with lots of dog-eared pages, then puts it back and takes down a red one.

Ava sighs again. "Our meeting should have started five minutes ago. Some of us are busy people.

We all have lives."

"I'm coming," Sarah says, as she flips through the red notebook. "Woohoo! This is the one!" She slides it in her backpack as the voice of doom fills the hall.

"You three need to hit the bricks!" Mrs. Frisner yells, a large dragon-and-unicorn tornado charging toward us.

Sarah grabs her backpack and the three of us hurry out the doors to the playground benches. It's where we always meet. Right now, it's just the three of us in KTMC. We tried advertising; Ava used to stick flyers in lockers until her dad got mad at her for using up two of his magenta ink cartridges because she printed so many. We tried snacks, too. We thought Ben Hinklemeyer was going to join, but it turns out he just wanted a cupcake. He left as soon as he had licked every last bit of icing from his cupcake wrapper—before the meeting even started. We have to work on our recruitment strategies. It's slow going, but we haven't given up hope.

"Bigfoot and science have NOTHING in common!" Ava says, popping a cashew from her homemade trail mix into her mouth.

"You have three whole days of science coming up next week," I remind her. "You'll eat, sleep, and breathe science at Peaceful Pine."

Ava closes her eyes and smiles. "That's right," she says. "That's what I need to keep telling myself. Now start the meeting!"

"I call to order this meeting of The Kids for Truth about Magical Creatures," I say. "We tackled unicorns in our first case. One Magical down, hundreds left to go. Which one do we investigate next?"

The three of us stare into space, thinking.

"Trolls?" Sarah suggests.

I shake my head. "They're only active when it's freezing. You know how hard it is to find a troll when it's above thirty degrees outside? What about ghosts?"

"Too hard to see," Sarah says. "Mermaids?"

"You're getting warmer," I say.

"Not mermaids!" Ava says. "All they do is sit on rocks and groom themselves." Then she makes her voice high and bubbly, like Mrs. Frisner's clock. "My name is Seaweed, and I'm a mermaid. I enjoy combing my hair with seashells and staring at shiny objects. It's FIN-tastic!" Ava's voice is normal again. "Please. Don't put us through that misery."

"We need to pick a Magical we can interview, like we did with our first case," I suggest.

"That'll give our investigation more credibility," Sarah says.

"And it's better for *Creature Feature*," I add.

"First-person research is important," Ava says.

"Especially if we want to get published in a scientific journal." She's always thinking ahead.

I look at my watch. "I have to get home soon. Let's each come up with three Magicals we'd like to investigate. We can decide at our next meeting."

"But no mermaids, right?" Ava asks.

Sarah sighs. "No mermaids. But it wouldn't hurt you to be a little more open-minded."

"My mind is open," Ava says. "But it's not empty… like a mermaid's."

Trolls are sounding better and better.

CHAPTER 3
THE WHEELS ON THE BUS

THE DAY WE LEAVE FOR OUR FIELD TRIP, MRS. Frisner goes over our goals. "We'll study native plants and observe wildlife. We have our microscopes and telescopes ready to go."

Then she calls out a long list of supplies; we each had to bring an item. Sarah brought baked beans. I brought bug spray, and Ava brought a twenty-four-pack of biodegradable toilet paper that she keeps squeezing in excitement. There's also a pile of Puffy Pals marshmallow bags as tall as I am stacked next to Mrs. Frisner's desk.

We grab seats at the very back of the bus. Ava sits next to me by the window. Unfortunately, Sarah's seatmate is the large pile of Puffy Pals marshmallows, and every time the bus hits a pothole, a bag or two land in her lap. Each bag has a green sticker with a note in Mrs. Frisner's handwriting: *Special project—not for campfire roasting.*

The bus's engine is so noisy Ava and I have to shout at each other instead of talk. I glance across the aisle at Sarah from time to time, and she has her sketch book out. Sarah is quiet sometimes; I think it's because she's an artist. She studies things—flowers, trees, people; she looks at how the light hits them at different times of the day. She takes the time to understand things, and I think that's why she's such a good friend. After more than two hours of sketching, she yells across to me and Ava, "I read a lot about Peaceful Pine State Park. You know what makes it so special?"

"It's *not* Mrs. Frisner's classroom," I offer.

She laughs. "No. The flying squirrels. Isn't that great? And get this—not only do they fly, they glow, too!"

"Flying, glowing squirrels," I say, "Are you sure they aren't Magicals?"

"No. They're Ordinaries," Sarah says. "They glow because of flower...uh...flori... something. I can't remember the word."

"Fluorescence," Ava shouts. "Flying squirrels are nocturnal—they're awake at night—so being able to glow helps them recognize each other in the dark." She says this like flying, glowing squirrels are something you talk about every day.

The bus makes a sharp turn, ka-thumping across a gravel parking lot and causing a Puffy Pals avalanche. It gives one last wheezing gasp and stops. The doors squeak open and a man in a tan shirt and brown pants gets on board. He's wearing a gold name badge that glints when the sun hits it.

"Boys and girls!" he yells. "Welcome to Peaceful Pine State Park!"

"It's not so peaceful now," Ava whispers.

The man hitches his left and right thumbs in his belt loops and rocks back and forth, heel to toe.

"I'm Ranger Joe Mills!" he shouts. "Before you get off the bus, we're gonna go over a few rules." Only it sounds more like ruuuuulzzzz.

"You are here to learrrrrrrrn!" he continues. "There will be no selfie-taking at Peaceful Pine!" The bus gets deathly silent. "There will be no flower-picking, no pebble-skipping, and no lollygagging, either."

Kids exchange terrified looks.

"Do you know why we have these rules?" he asks. "Because I am Ranger Joe Mills, and you are here to learrrrrrrrn!"

"More like Ranger No Thrills," Ava whispers.

We pile out of the bus and unload our equipment. There are infrared binoculars, something labeled BF NIGHT VISION GLASSES, and of course there are the marshmallows.

Ava looks suspicious. "Where are the telescopes

and microscopes?" she asks Mrs. Frisner. "And where are the flying squirrels?"

She has her camera ready to go. Ava loves macro photography—taking extremely close-up photos. Ever wonder what a moldy piece of bread looks like, up close and personal? I know, thanks to Ava's photos. I have a feeling I'll know what a moldy marshmallow looks like, too.

Mrs. Frisner snorts. "Squirrels? Who needs airborne rodents when we're searching for one of the greatest Magicals of all time!" As soon as she says it, a pinecone comes hurtling out of the nearest tree. It misses bonking her on the head by an inch.

The three of us don't have to say it; we know. This isn't a science field trip at all. It's an expedition to find Bigfoot.

Mrs. Frisner shares this news with our class, and there are whoops and hollers, but not from us or Madison Rainwater, who's standing nearby. Madison's new to our class this year and doesn't say much, but if you smile at her, she smiles back. She's always reading, too—books about plants and animals mostly. Her hiking boots have mud stains, and they look like she's worn them a lot. She picks up a bag of Puffy Pals. "It's not gonna work," she says under her breath. "He doesn't like marshmallows."

Ava, Sarah, and I look at each other. What does Madison Rainwater know that we don't?

CHAPTER 4

FLYING SQUIRRELS RULE, BIGFOOT DROOLS

OUR CAMPSITE IS A MILE AWAY. UPHILL. WHEN WE get there, a sea of army-green canvas bags are waiting for us.

"Bet you thought you'd get an easy, modern, press-a-button-and-the-whole-thing-assembles-itself kind of tent, didn't you? Used to sleeping on air mattresses, aren't you? Well, there is no *glamping* at Peaceful Pine!" Ranger Mills taps one of the canvas bags with his boot. "Everybody has a tent buddy. It's your job to assemble your tent together."

Nobody moves.

He claps twice. "Get a move on! Hard work is the camper's friend!"

I'm Brandon's tent buddy. Ava and Sarah are buddies, too, so we pitch our tents next to each other.

Brandon and I tip over our bag, and a canvas

sheet, metal poles, and wooden stakes fall out. If we can't figure out how to pitch our tent, at least we'll be able to kill any vampires that show up.

Ava and Sarah have their tent up first. Its poles are perfectly straight; a hurricane couldn't move their tent. Ours, on the other hand, looks like an elephant sat on top of it. It sags in the middle and the poles are crooked.

When our tent is finally up, Brandon decides to help Mrs. Frisner and Ranger Mills build the class campfire, so I call an emergency KTMC meeting.

"I know we haven't decided which Magical to investigate, but since we're here..." I say.

"Bigfoot?" Sarah asks.

"Bigfoot," Ava answers.

"We'll prove he's not as great as everyone thinks he is," I say.

"Here's the problem," Ava says. "There's no cell service here, and I doubt there's a library in one of these pine trees. So, how are we going to do our research?"

"Leave that to me," Sarah says. She sets off in the

direction of Mrs. Frisner, and ten minutes later, comes back with an armful of books, magazines, and articles printed from websites.

"How'd you do that?" I ask.

"I told Mrs. Frisner I'm a huge fan of Bigfoot, and I can't wait to find him, but I don't know how. She gave me these and told me to brush up on the big guy," Sarah says.

"Not exactly the truth, but not exactly a lie," I say.

She dumps the pile of books and articles in the middle of their tent, and we start reading. *The Definitive Guide to Bigfoot*; *From Snow to Swamp: Finding Bigfoot in Any Terrain*; *Squatch Watch: My Life Investigating Sasquatch*; *Big Shoes to Fill: A Bigfoot Biography*.

"Did you know he goes by over one hundred different names?" Sarah asks. "In Florida he's called Skunk Ape and in Texas he's Woolybooger."

"This article from Abominable.net says he's called Yowie in the Australian outback," Ava adds.

"This guy gets around," I say. "He's the Honey Island Swamp Monster in Louisiana."

"And lots of Native American tribes have different names for him, too," Sarah says, "Sasquatch is one of them."

"There's no way there's only *one* Bigfoot," I say. "No creature, no matter how magical, could be in so many places. That's the first thing we need to prove—there's not just one."

Sarah holds up the book she's reading so we can see the cover—*Bigfoot Throughout History*. "This says Bigfoot was there at the signing of the Declaration of Independence, and there's a chapter about him jousting with Henry VIII. He even flew with the Wright Brothers, according to this."

"C'mon," I say, "that's impossible."

"I agree," Ava says. "And what's up with him

hiding all the time? I guess when you're such a big deal, you don't have to show up for your fans. They should have to hunt for you, right?"

Ava holds up the latest edition of *Magical Monthly* with the headline "Where's Bigfoot? Magical Leads Fans on Giant Goose Chase."

"Hiding from your public doesn't make you special, it makes you rude," Sarah says. "Do you think movie stars would be so popular if they disappeared every time a fan asked for a selfie? KTMC should prove that Bigfoot's not worth the hype. Flying squirrels rule. Bigfoot drools."

"But we're forgetting the biggest point of all," Ava says. "Those feet. *Yeti Yearly* says Bigfoot can run faster and jump higher than any other Magical."

"Well I'm halfway through this article Frisner printed from *Garden Gnome News Online*, and it sounds like his big feet cause big problems," Sarah says. "They trample gardens and anything else that gets in their way. We'll prove that big feet are *not* a big deal."

We're quiet for a while as we all continue reading.

"Hey, did you guys see this?" Sarah says, breaking

the silence and holding up an article Mrs. Frisner printed from online. "It says the state was about to close Peaceful Pine for good because nobody was visiting anymore. They were going to sell the land to developers, but now attendance is through the roof. That's good at least, right?"

She hands the article over and Ava skims it. "Yeah, but it says here the squirrels have nothing to do with it."

"They're coming to see Bigfoot," I say.

"Exactly," Ava says, "and his fans are bringing their illegal campfires and litter with them. So the park's still open, but at what cost?"

"Poor squirrels," Sarah says.

"Poor Peaceful Pine. Period," I say.

A loud clanging interrupts us. Ranger No Thrills is banging a large metal triangle with a stick. "Come and get it! You take what you get, and you eat what you take!" His shouts are followed by Mrs. Frisner's cackle.

This is going to be a long three days.

CHAPTER 5
KINDA SQUIRRELY

I CAN'T SLEEP BECAUSE BRANDON'S SNORING SOUNDS like Darth Vader with a head cold, so I count the number of times a gnat tries to fly up my nose. I'm up to thirteen when I feel the footsteps. They're soft at first, but they get louder. Something is walking toward our tent, and whatever it is, it's huge, because the ground is shaking.

It's getting closer. Closer. It grunts right next to our tent. A bear? I don't move. I hear a low whisper. The voice is so deep the tent vibrates. A higher-pitched whisper answers it. They go back and forth until the voices stop. Footsteps again, getting farther and farther away.

I peek my head out of the tent, and Ava's peeking out, too.

"You heard that?" she whispers.

"How could I *not* hear that?" I whisper back.

Looking past Ava's tent, I see a small figure

standing on the edge of the woods waving at something disappearing into the trees. I squint as hard as I can. It's Madison Rainwater.

"I'll get Sarah," Ava says.

I grab my shoes and put them on outside their tent.

"Mmmph. Leave me alone," Sarah mumbles. "I like riding my unicycle with penguins."

"Wake up!" Ava whispers. "C'mon!"

Ava grabs her camera, and Sarah is still half-asleep but manages to put on her yellow ducky bedroom slippers.

When Madison turns around, the three of us are standing there. "Oh!" she gasps. Her eyes are wide, and she studies us for a second. "I...uh...I think I was sleep walking," she says. "Where am I?"

She doesn't wait for us to tell her. She scurries off back to her tent.

"Who do you *really* think she was talking to?" Ava asks.

"The same creature who doesn't like Puffy Pals marshmallows—Bigfoot," Sarah answers.

A pinecone comes hurtling out of the tree next to us and bonks Ava on the head. "Ow! Peaceful Pine, my foot."

From one of the tallest branches, a high-pitched voice shouts, "Bigfoot, Big DEAL!"

We look up and a small, gray squirrel with a faint pink glow comes gliding down on what look like wings. He lands on the ground next to us, puts his paws on his hips, and taps his foot impatiently.

"I suppose you're like all the rest of them?" he says, poking the toe of Sarah's yellow ducky slipper. The duck's head bobs up and down.

"The rest of who?" I ask.

"His paparazzi!" the squirrel shouts. "Flashbulbs going at all hours of the night. Video cameras all over the park. Nobody gives two twigs about flying squirrels anymore!"

Sarah shakes her foot to get him to stop poking her duck. "What's your name?" she asks.

"Earl," he answers, twitching his tail.

"Your name is Earl Squirrel?" Sarah says.

"So? What's it to ya, lady?" Earl says.

"Why did your parents do that to you?" Sarah asks, and I can't tell if she's about to laugh or cry.

"Whaddya mean?" Earl answers. "Merle and Pearl Squirrel are fine folks."

"Never mind," Sarah says to herself, holding back a laugh.

"Hold on!" I say, trying to get us back on topic. "Weren't you saying something about Bigfoot being bad for the park?"

"Oh, bad doesn't even begin to describe it, buster," Earl says. "Life was good here until *he* moved in. Suddenly a flying squirrel ain't nothing compared to a guy with feet the size of tractor tires. I glow in the dark and fly, for Pete's sake. What more do they want?"

"Wellll," Ava says, "technically, you don't fly. You glide. You have flaps of skin between your arms and legs that work like a parachute. It only looks like you're flying."

"Hey, who's the squirrel here, lady? I know what I do!" Earl's paws are on his hips again. "And technically, you're a know-it-all," he mutters.

"It's a big forest," Sarah says, yawning. "It just seems like there's plenty of room for everybody."

"Yeah, well, you tell yourself that the next time someone throws their empty tin cans in *your* yard. Or sets fire to your favorite shrub because they didn't put their campfire out the right way," Earl says. His voice catches when he says *shrub* and his lower lip trembles. "I loved that shrub. It had little purple blossoms in the summer. I would crawl under its branches to get away from it all." His tail droops. "But now it's gone. All gone. Thanks to you-know-who."

"That's awful!" Ava says. "What kind of terrible creature would sit back and let his fans do so much harm?"

"A big tyrant!" I say.

"Wait!" Sarah says. Her right eyebrow is raised, which means she's not happy. "If we're going to investigate Bigfoot, we have to be fair. This is one side of the story."

"Yeah," Earl says. "The right side!"

Sarah ignores him. "We need to gather evidence from *both* sides," she says to me and Ava and then turns back to Earl. "We're The Kids for Truth about Magical Creatures. We're trying to prove that Ordinaries are every bit as special as Magicals. Can we interview you and your friends for our blog? I think we can help, if you let us."

Earl rubs his chin and thinks. "Will I get my picture taken?" he asks.

"Definitely," Ava says.

"Can I wear my sunglasses? Celebrities wear sunglasses in photos," Earl says.

"Uh...well...our blog is on the scientific side," Ava says. "No sunglasses."

He thinks again. "Okay. But I get to approve the photos."

Ava sighs. "It's a deal."

"Meet me tomorrow night. Same time. Same place," Earl says. "And don't be late. Frank gets nervous when people are late."

"Who's Frank?" Ava asks, but Earl doesn't answer as he scampers back up the tree.

The three of us head back to our tents. Brandon is still snoring, and the gnat still tries to fly up my nose, but it's not all bad. We have an interview tomorrow— great practice for my future as a journalist. Plus, we're going to prove Bigfoot is a big dud, and *that* will be the story of the year!

CHAPTER 6

NOW YOU SEE HIM, NOW YOU DON'T

"RISE AND SHINE, CAMPERS!" RANGER MILLS IS walking down our row of tents yelling at the top of his lungs.

A big cauldron of clumpy oatmeal sits in the middle of the campfire. As we file past, Mrs. Frisner gives each of us a heaping scoop. I stick my plastic spoon in the middle and it doesn't move, like the flag Neil Armstrong planted on the moon. Ava is sculpting hers into what I think is a walrus—maybe a manatee.

Mrs. Frisner has a collapsible red wagon overflowing with Puffy Pals marshmallow bags. She wheels it around the campfire, giving each student two bags. Ava gives me her "we're not going to like this" look.

"Everybody, read the back of your bags," Mrs.

Frisner rasps. "Our expedition is about to begin!"

I turn mine over. WANT TO FIND BIGFOOT? HERE'S HOW! It says in giant red letters. In smaller print underneath, there are instructions:

Know what Bigfoot likes best? That's right—**marshmallows**! And there's no marshmallow better than a **Puffy Pals** marshmallow! Leave a trail of **Puffy Pals**, and Bigfoot will come to YOU!

Plus, send us your picture with Bigfoot, and we'll put *you* on a bag of **Puffy Pals**, too!

I look around the campfire; everybody's smiling and giving each other high fives. But not me. Or Ava. Or Sarah. Or Madison Rainwater, for that matter.

"Class, Ranger Mills would like to say a few words," Mrs. Frisner says.

"Boys and gurrrrrlz," he says, thumbs in belt loops again. "For years, Peaceful Pine was the most visited park in the state. We had to turn people away, until folks got so busy they couldn't be bothered with the great outdoors. Spending all their time on newfangled electronic devices. The state was going to close the park until something BIG happened. Seems Bigfoot decided to make the park his home, and now we can't keep people away."

No Thrills rocks back and forth. "We haven't seen him, but we *do* have evidence. Trampled campfires. Squashed video cameras. And *this*!" He holds up a photo of a footprint that's easily two feet long. "That's not from a squirrel, my friends!" he says, and Mrs. Frisner cackles.

"Now, you might think all this foot traffic can't be good for the park," Ranger Mills continues. "And you're right. We're overrun with litterbugs and illegal campfires, but we'll figure out how to deal with that. Our biggest problem is folks looking for Bigfoot and never finding him. If people start to think he left the park, they'll stop coming back.

"Your mission!" Ranger Mills barks. "Help us find Bigfoot and keep the park open!" Mrs. Frisner nods in agreement like she's all for protecting the park, but I have a sneaking suspicion she just wants her face on the back of a Puffy Pals bag.

Ranger Mills passes out maps of the park, and Ava, Sarah, and I look at ours. "You'll find your group's section of trail highlighted in orange. You place one marshmallow every fifty feet." He claps twice. "Time's a'wastin'! Get goin'!"

Ava holds a bag of Puffy Pals in each hand. "This isn't science. We're surrounded by raccoons and coyotes. These aren't going to make it to lunchtime."

After a day of making marshmallow trails, we drag ourselves to the campfire for dinner.

"What is this?" Sarah says, poking at her supper with her plastic fork.

"I think it's a hotdog," I say.

"Maybe in its previous life," she says and continues to poke.

I shovel a heaping spoonful of beans in my mouth. Big mistake.

"They're cold," I say to anyone who will listen. "How can beans that have been sitting on a campfire for an hour be cold?"

"Mrs. Frisner made them," Sarah says. "Her icy heart got too close to the beans."

"Class, before we get to the campfire stories," Mrs. Frisner says, "Ranger Mills would like to say a few words."

He steps forward and stares us down. "Tonight, I'm going to address an important topic," he says. "Toilets. There are some ruuuuuulz we need to follow concerning the camp toilets."

We listen while Ranger Mills tells us how to flush the camp toilets, how to clean the camp toilets, and how to not stop up the camp toilets. By now, it's dark outside, and Mrs. Frisner's nodded off against a big rock. Every once in a while, her head bobs. We never get to the stories; after an hour of toilets, Ranger Mills sends us to bed.

We change into our pajamas for lights-out. Brandon's already snoring when I look at my watch. It's time.

Ava and Sarah climb out of their tent and the three of us make our way to Earl's tree. He's there with his friends—an opossum on one side and a raccoon on the other. The opossum takes one look at Sarah's ducky bedroom slippers, becomes stiff as a board, and falls over. Dead as a doornail.

"Aaagh!" the raccoon shouts and clutches his chest. "Loretta! Oh, Loretta!" he says standing over the opossum. "We never said goodbye!" He buries his face in his paws.

"She's not *really* dead, Frank," Earl mutters out of the corner of his mouth. "It's her defense mechanism. She's only *playing* dead. Opossums do that. We talked about this."

"We did?!" Frank looks up, takes a deep breath, and nods. "You're right. We did." He wipes his forehead with the back of his paw. "Smell the roses, Frank," he says to himself as he takes a deep breath in. "Cool the hot chocolate," he says as he blows the deep breath out.

Not moving a muscle, Loretta asks, "Are the ducks real?"

"No," Sarah says. "They're stuffed."

Loretta sits up. "My great-great-grandfather is stuffed," she says. "He's in the natural history museum."

Earl clears his throat. "Frank, Loretta, I'd like to introduce you to…uh…" He's scratching his head, trying to remember who we are. "Three nosey kids," he finally says. "They want to interview us about Bigfoot."

At the mention of Bigfoot's name, Loretta stiffens and falls over again.

"Oh no! Loretta! Gone too soon!" Frank says, raising his clenched paws and shaking them at the heavens.

"She's not dead, Frank! How many times do we hafta go over this?" Earl asks.

Frank smells the roses and cools the hot chocolate, and Loretta opens her eyes.

"Why are you so upset about Bigfoot?" I ask Earl, getting the ball rolling.

"Wouldn't you be? I was the star of the show until that oversized hairball moved in!"

"But…" Loretta says, trying to get a word in.

"People came from miles around. *Miles*, I tell you! All to see the flying squirrels. No more. Now they wouldn't care if I flew in on a spaceship!"

"Earl, dear…" Loretta trails off.

"What about you, Frank?" Ava asks. "Why do you hate Bigfoot?"

Frank wrings his little paws. "Not hate," he says. "I don't *hate* Bigfoot. Heck, I don't even know the guy personally." He takes a deep breath. "Look. I'm a raccoon, right? I don't fly. I don't play dead. I eat people's garbage. That's my superpower. And we used to get some gooooood garbage at Peaceful Pine. High-quality stuff, you know? Salmon. Chicken kababs.

The occasional steak. It was heaven for a raccoon. Until Bigfoot came along."

"Frank, dear, you know there hasn't been…" Loretta begins, but Frank keeps talking.

"Now even the garbage is garbage. Fast food wrappers. Deep-fried junk. Marshmallows. Don't get me started on the marshmallows. It's enough to make a raccoon despair."

"Why is that Bigfoot's fault?" Sarah asks.

"Nobody has time to plan a camping trip anymore. They're too busy rushing to get a picture of the world's greatest hide-and-seek champion to think about their dinner—or mine," Frank says, wringing his paws again. "They come in for the day with their electronic gadgets. They hit the fast food drive-through, then they hit the park. The trouble is, they leave all their junk behind when they go."

Frank starts smelling the roses and cooling the hot chocolate again while Ava snaps photos and Sarah takes detailed notes. I'm beginning to get a better picture of the trouble Bigfoot is causing Peaceful Pine.

Everybody is quiet for a minute, and I look up; the full moon has moved across the sky. "We should get back to camp," I say. "We've got some good information thanks to the three of you."

Earl nods. "Glad we're good for *something!*"

"Wait!" Sarah says. "We haven't really heard from Loretta."

"Don't worry," Loretta says. "I'm nocturnal. You can find me any time after nine p.m."

Earl, Frank, and Loretta scuttle up the nearest pine tree, and we begin the trek back to camp. Ava zips up her camera case and stops.

"Do you hear that?" she asks.

It's the same low whispering we heard the night before. There's a clearing in the trees, and in the light of the full moon we see two figures sitting on a fallen log. One is Madison Rainwater. The other has to be ten feet tall when he's standing. It's hard to see details, but I can tell he's covered in thick fur. His feet are the biggest I've ever seen—almost the size of car tires.

Madison is peeling a clementine, and she hands

Bigfoot a slice. It's the size of a dime in his enormous hand. They go back and forth—a slice for Madison, a slice for Bigfoot, until it's all gone. They whisper back and forth and Madison puts her hand in his. There's a flash of bright, white light, and they're gone. Poof! Disappeared into thin air.

"Okay. I'm not the only one who saw that, right?" Ava asks.

"Nope. I think we all did," I answer. "And I bet we're all thinking the same thing."

"Where'd they go?" asks Sarah.

"Exactly," I say.

CHAPTER 7

ONE IS THE LONELIEST NUMBER

WE TURN TOWARD CAMP, WHEN THERE'S ANOTHER flash of light. We look back. Madison and Bigfoot are sitting on the log, but this time Madison is wearing something metal with horns.

"Is that…" Ava begins.

"A Viking helmet?" Sarah finishes. "Where'd they get it? The gift shop?"

"Why would they sell *that* at a state park?" Ava asks. "Sunscreen, yes. Viking helmets, no."

Madison reaches into her backpack, pulls out another clementine, and hands it to Bigfoot. He pops the whole thing in his mouth, chomps a few times, then gives a big smile. His teeth are covered by the rind, and his smile is completely orange. Madison's laughter echoes through the woods. Then Bigfoot stands, and in three huge, earth-shaking bounds, he disappears into the trees.

We're frozen in place. Madison is walking toward us, but even with the full moon, in the shadows of the forest, she doesn't see us until she almost bumps into Sarah.

"Oh!" She stares wide-eyed like the night before. "I...uh...I think I was sleep-walking again," she mutters.

The heads of Sarah's ducky slippers bob up and down as she moves closer to Madison. "We saw everything. The light. The helmet. The big feet. We're trying to figure out what's going on so we can help the park. We could use your help, too. Please."

Madison keeps her eyes glued on Sarah, studying her. "If I tell you, you'll help him?"

"We'll do our best," Sarah says. "But until we know what's going on, we can't promise anything."

Madison nudges a pinecone with the toe of her sneaker. "Okay. But you *do* have to promise not to tell Mrs. Frisner or Ranger Mills."

"That's a promise we can make," I say, and she begins her story.

"My family goes camping every summer, and this year we came to Peaceful Pine. We brought our kayaks—me, my older brother, Mom, and Dad. We took them out on Bent Knee River. It rained the night before," Madison goes on. "The river was really high, and the water was rushing, but we kayak a lot, so we thought it was safe. Mom and Dad put their boats in first, then David, then me, and everything was great until we hit rapids. I hit a boulder in the river, and it tipped my kayak." Madison stops, kicking the pinecone.

"It's okay. Go on," Sarah says.

"By the time my family realized I wasn't behind

them, they were too far away to see me. My boat was swept down river. I went under a couple of times and swallowed water. I could barely breathe. I grabbed on to a big rock in the middle of the river and held on as tight as I could, but my fingers slipped, and I couldn't hold on anymore. I closed my eyes and let go, and that's when it happened."

"What?" Ava and Sarah ask at the same time.

"Big, gentle hands scooped me up and carried me to the other side of the river, where my parents were looking for me. I didn't realize it was Bigfoot until I opened my eyes. Now I'm always sure to spend time with him when my family takes trips to Peaceful Pine. *You* know Bigfoot from the Puffy Pals bags and Mrs. Frisner, but *I* know the real one," Madison says.

"And speaking of *one*," Ava says, "there can't be only *one* Bigfoot. There's a whole herd of Big…feet, right?"

Madison shakes her head. "There's only one, but he has special…" She pauses. "Abilities."

"But if there's only one," Ava says, "how could he be in so many places throughout history? There's no way the same guy could help build the pyramids *and* cross the Delaware with George Washington."

A big smile spreads across Madison's face, and a lightbulb goes on in my mind.

"He's a time traveler," I say. "A really big, really rude time traveler. That explains the whole 'Find me if you can!' thing. And the Viking helmet."

"That's right," Madison says. "Except the rude part. He doesn't mean to cause so much trouble. He's shy—like me. He's trying to help."

"Help!" Ava says. "How is he helping? No one cares about the flying squirrels anymore, or any of the other Ordinaries."

"The park was in trouble anyway," Madison says. "People stopped coming to see the squirrels *before* Bigfoot came. That's why he's here."

"Explain," Ava says, "because so far this isn't making any sense."

"He thinks the Ordinaries are amazing. He came to talk with them, help them get noticed again. It backfired."

"How so?" Ava asks.

"One night he went to his favorite clearing in the

woods to look at the stars," Madison continues. "But someone had pitched a tent there. Before he could get away, the guy took a picture. It's blurry, and he looks like a big, furry blob walking in the woods, but that's all it took. Word got out and the visitors came back, but they brought their video cameras, their litter, and illegal campfires with them. They're here for Bigfoot. He's trying to figure out how to fix it."

"He's not doing a very good job," Ava says under her breath.

"His heart is as big as his feet," Madison says. "He puts out dangerous campfires, picks up litter, puts baby birds back in their nests. He doesn't mean to bring attention to himself. It's hard when you're so... so... BIG!"

"While we're talking about big," Sarah cuts in, "what's so special about those feet? I mean, Julian has big feet, and nobody cares about those."

I ignore that comment.

"They're not just big, they're how he travels," Madison says.

"Yeah, we get that," I say.

"Through time," Madison adds.

I finally see the whole picture. "So... his big feet are more like... big shuttles," I say.

"And if you step in one of his footprints while it's still fresh, *you* can time travel, too," Madison adds.

Thoughts race through my brain. "So...if he can travel through time...he can change history?"

"No." Madison shakes her head. "He can't change the past, only visit."

"There's only one way to know if any of this is true." Sarah looks at me and Ava. "We need to talk with him. Can we?" she asks Madison.

"Will you be kind? He's sensitive," Madison says.

"We'll try our best," Sarah says again.

Madison toes another pinecone while she's thinking. "Meet me at the log at three p.m. tomorrow," she finally says. "It's his favorite place in the forest. I can't promise anything."

"Understood," I say. "And thank you."

When we get back to camp and climb inside our tents, I close my eyes to dream, but I think I'm already in one.

CHAPTER 8
CRISSCROSS APPLESAUCE

THE NEXT DAY, AFTER OUR LUNCH OF REHEATED chili, we make our way to the park's "classroom." It's a small cinderblock building right next to the bathrooms, and Ava holds her nose as she walks inside. We sit on the last bench closest to the door.

Ranger Mills stands in front of our class, thumbs in belt loops, rocking heel to toe. "Class, what's the single most important piece of equipment you have as a camper?" he asks.

Brandon raises his hand. "Your tent?"

"Wrong!" Ranger Mills says.

"A first-aid kit?" Jenny Albright asks.

"Wrong!" Mills yells.

"A stove, pots, and food?" Justin Polaski says.

"Wrong, wrong, and wrong." Ranger Mills crosses his arms. No other hands go up. "SHOELACES! You won't get far as a camper without the right shoelaces."

I glance down at Ava's notebook. She's written *Not Science* and underlined it. "Sorry," I mouth.

There's a drawing of a shoelace on the old chalkboard that's bolted to the wall. Ranger Mills picks up a wooden yardstick. "Let's start with aglets," he says, and slaps the yardstick against the illustrated shoelace, pointing to its metal tip. "A good aglet can save your life!"

I look around. The classroom is so hot that Mrs. Frisner's glasses are fogged up. It doesn't seem to bother her, though; she's still underlining passages in *Bigfoot, His Life in Politics.* The clock on the wall reads 2:50 p.m., and Madison slips out the door when Ranger Mills turns his back. One by one, Ava, Sarah, and I follow.

At the log, Madison cups her hands to her mouth and makes noises that sound like birdcall. "Chir, chirrup, chirrup. Chir, chirrup, chirrup." Then she picks up a nearby stick and knocks three times on the fallen log. Three knocks answer from nearby. She knocks again. Three knocks answer from closer this time.

Ava starts to say something, but Madison stops

her and whispers, "Be quiet. You'll frighten him."

"He's ten feet tall, and *we're* going to frighten *him*?" Ava whispers.

Sticks crunch nearby, and Madison keeps whistling until the branches part just enough to see a large pair of dark eyes looking at us.

"It's okay," Madison lets him know. "They're friends of mine. They won't hurt you." She holds out her hand.

"Friends?" Bigfoot says in a low, deep whisper.

"Friends." Madison smiles.

The branches part a little bit more and an enormous foot comes out of the trees and lands right on top of a small pine sapling.

Bigfoot gasps. "Sorry, little guy!"

His hands are almost as big as his feet, and he struggles to get the sapling to stand up straight again. Madison takes the shoelace off her left sneaker, and he wraps it around the sapling's trunk where it bent.

"There, there," Bigfoot says, patting the little tree the way you pat a puppy or a little kid's head. "All better now."

I guess Ranger No Thrills was onto something with the shoelaces.

Madison takes Bigfoot by the hand and leads him over. The ground shakes with every step he takes, but I notice something else, too. Bright orange flowers sprout up where he stood next to the sapling—flowers that didn't exist a minute ago.

"Why don't we sit down?" Madison says.

"Crisscross applesauce?" Bigfoot asks, and Madison nods. "I like applesauce. On pizza."

"Ewwwww!" Ava says. "Are you kid—" But she's cut short when Bigfoot accidentally steps on her foot.

Ava's cheeks fill with air as she takes a deep breath. "Ow, ow, ow!" she yells, grabbing her left foot and hopping up and down.

Bigfoot gasps again, and when she stops hopping, he reaches out like she's a sapling and pats her head. "Sorry," he says, "all better now."

Ava purses her lips, then opens her mouth to say something when Madison speaks up. "This is Ava Chen," she says, and Bigfoot smiles. Ava doesn't waste time. She folds her arms and tilts her head the

way she does when she
doesn't believe something.
"You time travel?" she
asks.

Bigfoot nods.

"How? Radio waves?
Quantum physics?"

Bigfoot looks puzzled. "I
clear my mind and think of
where I want to go."

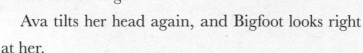

Ava tilts her head again, and Bigfoot looks right
at her.

"Science can't explain everything," he says.

Ava's eyes widen. "Can you hear my thoughts?"

Bigfoot shakes his head. "No, but I *can* feel your
energy. Your head is full of a lot of… stuff," he says.
"Always buzzing. Like a beehive. You need to relax.
You're very tense."

"Serious," Ava corrects him. "Not tense."

"Seriously tense," Bigfoot answers.

There's an awkward silence. The only sound is
Sarah's pencil as she sketches Bigfoot, until I ask,

"Can we take a few pictures?" but before Ava can get her camera ready, Bigfoot stands, sticks his nose in the air, and sniffs.

"Smell that?" he asks.

The only scent I pick up is Bigfoot, who smells like a *really* big, *really* wet Labrador retriever multiplied by ten, but we all shake our heads.

"Smoke," he says, standing up. "The forest needs my help!"

And in three enormous bounds, he's gone.

CHAPTER 9
FREE YOUR MIND

IT'S CAMPER'S DELIGHT FOR DINNER. THAT'S WHAT Mrs. Frisner calls leftover hotdogs cut into chunks and mixed in with leftover beans. For dessert, we have snack-sized cans of fruit cocktail.

"Sixty percent real fruit," Sarah reads from the label. "What's the other forty percent?" Me and Ava shrug. Like the building of the pyramids, some mysteries will never be solved.

We're still pondering when Mrs. Frisner tells us it's time to check our marshmallow trails for signs of Bigfoot, and as soon as our class is on the move, we hang back and head in the opposite direction.

When we reach the fallen log, Madison knocks and we wait. Soon, the branches part like before and Bigfoot appears.

Right away, Ava blurts, "So, this time-travel stuff. It's a trick, right? Smoke and mirrors?"

"Ava!" Sarah says.

"What?" Ava says. "There's no sense beating around the bush. Might as well get to the point."

"No trick," Bigfoot says. "You have to clear your mind. When your mind is at peace, you can go anywhere. Do anything. That's easier for some than others." He raises an eyebrow at her.

"That makes no sense. If everyone could do this time-travel thing, we wouldn't need airports," Ava says, looking satisfied with herself.

Bigfoot nods. "People are too busy to clear their minds. Always running. That's what Nessie says."

"Wait," Sarah says. "Nessie? As in—the Loch Ness Monster. That Nessie?"

Bigfoot nods. "She's a good friend. Throws great parties."

Ava groans. "You have *got* to be kidding!"

Bigfoot whispers, "Follow me."

We follow him through the forest, climbing up, up, up until we come to Geezer Ledge—the highest point in Peaceful Pine State Park. Ranger Mills told us it got that name because it looks like the face of an old man.

We gaze out over the treetops and watch an eagle circle, hunting for dinner. The Bent Knee River winds its way across the park and disappears into a waterfall. I watch Sarah taking in the whole scene; I can practically see the painting coming together in her mind.

Ava snaps a few photos of Bigfoot, who's standing with his toes on the edge of Geezer Ledge; he closes his eyes and stretches out his arms, the wind blowing through his fur. He looks completely at peace. There's a giant flash of light. He's gone.

Madison smiles, and two seconds later, he's back, clutching a large, yellowed piece of paper. It's a sketch of some sort of flying machine. There's a bucket seat for a pilot to sit in and giant wooden wings like a bird's.

"Leonardo asked me to give this to you," Bigfoot says, handing the paper to Ava.

Sarah leans over Ava's shoulder, staring at the sketch. "Leonardo... da Vinci?"

"No. Leonardo Schwartz," Ava says. "Yes, Leonardo da Vinci. Look—he signed it."

Sarah leans over and runs her fingers over the signature. "He's one of my favorite artists. His use of light is extraordinary."

Bigfoot continues. "He also said to tell you that the world is full of science *and* magic. Just because one exists doesn't mean the other can't, too."

Before Ava can answer, a pinecone hurtles out of the nearest tree and bonks her on the head. We look up, and there's Earl, paws on his hips.

"Hey!" Ava shouts. "Why me? Why can't you aim at one of *them* once in a while?"

"Traitors!" Earl yells, scampering down the tree, with Frank and Loretta right behind him. "We know whose side you're on!"

Frank and Loretta hold picket signs—BIGFOOT IS A BIG PAIN! and BIGFOOT IS NO SMALL PROBLEM!

I look over at the big guy. His bottom lip is quivering, and there's a tear in the corner of his left eye. Before any of us can say a word, he does what Bigfoot does best—disappears. He runs into the forest, leaving a trail of bright yellow flowers and wet-dog stink behind.

CHAPTER 10
RUNNING OUT OF TIME

"OH NO!" MADISON SAYS. "WE HAVE TO FIND HIM!" She takes off running through the woods after Bigfoot, with Sarah and Ava right behind.

"Stay here," I tell Earl, "we'll be right back." And I take off, too.

A Bigfoot print is right in front of Madison; as her foot lands there's a blinding flash of light, and she disappears.

There's another flash, and Sarah's gone, then Ava.

When my foot lands in the print, the white light surrounds me. I'm hurtling through a kind of tunnel.

Lights whiz past until we all land on our backs with thuds.

I lift my head a little, trying to catch my breath, and see the flying machine from the sketch in the middle of a dusty room. A man with a long white beard stands over us, peering down.

"Leonardo," Madison says, standing up. She seems to know him. "Have you seen him?"

"Nathaniel?" the old guy asks and Madison nods.

He points to some extremely large footprints on the floor. Someone stepped in paint and left a trail.

"He went to his thinking place," Leonardo answers.

"Thanks," Madison says. "I wish we could stay longer, but we have to find him." The old man nods and pats her arm.

"Next time," he says.

"We have to go! Grab hands," Madison tells us. "I don't want us to get separated." Her foot lands in Bigfoot's print just as Ava wonders aloud, "Are you Leonardo da Vinci? The *real* one?"

The man with the white beard smiles before the lights start whizzing past again. We hurtle through time, and my stomach drops the way it does when you go downhill on a roller coaster.

Sarah shouts, "Who's Nathaniel?"

"Bigfoot!" Madison shouts back. "He doesn't like that name, though. He likes Nate. Leonardo's a formal kind of guy, so he calls him Nathaniel."

Before I can brace myself, we land with another thud. I'm staring up at an apple tree. One falls off and bonks Ava on the head.

"Why is it always me?" she mutters as we all sit up.

A man with long, wavy gray hair looks surprised to see us.

"Sorry, Isaac," Madison says. "I don't have this 'steering through time' thing down yet. Have you seen him?"

"Thinking place," the man says pointing at huge, muddy footprints under the tree, and Madison nods.

Ava looks from the apple tree to the man. "Isaac... Sir Isaac Newton?" she asks. "You developed the law of gravity!"

"I'm working on it," he says, looking at the apple tree, then back at Ava just as Madison steps in one of Bigfoot's muddy prints.

We're hurtling through time again, taking a sharp left turn, then a right. When we land this time, it's on a sandy beach. A woman with dark hair and a notebook sits nearby. The dress she's wearing looks like ones I've seen in photographs of my grandma from the 1960s.

"Madison!" she calls, giving her a big smile. "Did you take a wrong turn at Albuquerque?"

"Hi, Ms. Carson," Madison answers. "We're trying to get to his thinking place."

The woman points at a trail of humongous footsteps in the sand, and at the same time, Ava starts tugging on my arm.

"That's…that's…Do you know who that is?" she says. "That's Rachel Carson!" She waits for me to say something. "The marine biologist," she adds. "The famous author. The conservationist."

Before I can say anything, Ms. Carson is shaking our hands, introducing herself. As she shakes Ava's, my friend's cheeks turn red and she blurts, "Happy so to you meet I am!"

Ava turns even redder and takes a deep breath.

"What are you working on?" she asks, finally finding her words.

"Right now, I'm just watching and listening." Ms. Carson motions toward the sea. "It's amazing the things you learn when you slow down long enough to *really* look and listen," she says.

Madison's foot lands in one of Nate's prints. Suddenly the sea is gone and so is Rachel Carson, and we're back in the time tunnel.

"Bingo!" Madison says when we land this time.

We're surrounded by ferns, and a dragonfly the size of a pigeon lands on Sarah's shoulder. "Where are we?" she whispers.

A Pterodactyl soars overhead.

"The Jurassic period," Madison says. "Nate comes here when he needs to sort things out."

We follow Madison through more ferns and tall grass until we reach a shady spot where Nate sits crisscross applesauce with his eyes closed. He's humming; it's low and steady.

"What's he doing?" I ask Madison.

"Meditating," she whispers.

Nate opens one eye, then both. "Why did you follow me?" he asks in a low rumble.

"Because you can't run away every time something bad happens," Madison says. "We want you to come back."

"Why? I'll just mess up again." Nate stands up and wet-dog smell washes over us. I think Ava wants to hold her nose, but she's trying to be polite.

"Mistakes are how we learn—do you think any of the famous scientists we met on our way here made their discoveries on the first try?" Sarah says.

"I never thought I'd say this," Ava says, "but Sarah's right. You're trying to save the park; now we need to put our heads together and come up with a plan."

"Exactly," I say. "Talking with Earl and his friends would be a good start. They need to know why you're *really* at Peaceful Pine."

"Yeah," Sarah says. "They think you want the attention, that you like being in the spotlight."

"That's not true!" Nate says and tears well up in his eyes.

"We know that," I say. "But Earl and his friends don't. Talk to them."

"Come back," Madison says. "Please. The forest needs you. Earl and his friends need you, too." She holds her hand out toward Nate. He pauses a second, thinking, then places his enormous hand in hers. He reaches his other hand toward the rest of us, and we grab hold.

We land with a thud in one of Nate's footprints, surrounded by those bright yellow flowers. "Where did these come from?" Ava asks. "They weren't here when we left."

"They're from Nate's footprints," Madison says. "He might trample some things accidentally, but he always leaves new life behind."

"That little tidbit wasn't in that article you read from *Garden Gnome News Online*," Ava says to Sarah.

"I only read the first half," Sarah mumbles. Ava looks horrified. "I know. I know. I forgot to read the rest. Hey! Look at these flowers! They would make a beautiful painting," she says, changing the subject.

Earl, Loretta, and Frank are still waiting, waving their picket signs.

Sarah walks ahead of us, always the peacemaker. "I'd like you to meet someone special," she says to Earl, Frank, and Loretta. "Earl, this is Nate. Nate, this is Earl Squirrel and his friends Frank and Loretta."

Loretta gazes up at all ten feet of Nate. Her legs stiffen, her eyes close, and down she goes.

"Aaagh!" Frank yells, his paws flying up to his cheeks. "Alas, poor Loretta. I knew her, Earl!"

"Here we go again," Earl mutters to himself.

"Smell the roses, Frank," Sarah whispers. "She's only *playing* dead, remember?"

Loretta opens her eyes.

"Oh, my friend! You came back to us!" Frank cries, throwing his arms around her neck.

"Earl," Sarah says, "have you ever talked to Nate?"

Earl folds his arms and twitches his tail. "Nope! What for?"

"Because it's amazing the things you learn when you slow down long enough to *really* look and listen," Ava says.

We all stare at her. "What?" she says. "A wise woman told me that."

"Okay, then. Look, buster," Earl says, poking Nate's toe. "We were the main attraction until you moved in!"

"Earl, dear," Loretta says, "you know that's not true. Nobody visited Peaceful Pine anymore *until* Bigfoot came."

Earl is silent, looking off in the distance for what feels like forever. His lower lip trembles. "You're right, Loretta," he finally whispers, and she lays her paw on his shoulder.

"That's why I'm here," Nate says. "Everybody needs to remember how amazing you all are."

"We're Ordinaries," Earl says. "Nothing special. Not a Magical bone in my glowing body."

Nate shakes his head. "You don't understand. I can time travel, but I *can't* glow in the dark," he says to Earl, "or play dead," he says to Loretta, "or...or...be a raccoon," he says to Frank, who quietly blushes. "You're every bit as magical as I am, just in different ways."

"You really think so?" Earl asks, standing a little taller.

"I do," Nate answers.

Earl scratches his head. "Hey, wait a minute! She called you Nate. Your name's not Bigfoot?"

"That's right. Short for Nature Guardian. My friends call me Nate. I hope you will, too." He smiles down at Earl.

"This is nice, but we're all busy people," Ava says. "We all have lives. Let's get to work on that plan."

We all sit in a circle and brainstorm ways to save the park.

"We need to keep people coming in," I say.

"But get them to stop creating such a mess," Sarah adds.

"Let's hold a talent show!" Earl says. "I sing a lovely rendition of 'Wind Beneath My Wings.'"

"Why don't we keep brainstorming?" Loretta says.

Madison suggests park cleanup days. Ava mentions research groups helping out.

We sit for a minute until Nate breaks the silence. "I'm good at hiding, right?"

We all nod.

"What about a scavenger hunt?" he says.

I see Ava's wheels turning. "And people have to learn about nature to figure out the clues!"

Madison frowns. "But do you want people to actually find you, Nate?"

"No, but if they're polite, and quiet, and respect the forest, they might see my foot. Or hand. Or elbow. Enough to know I'm here and hopefully they'll come back."

"It's perfect," Sarah says, and we all agree.

"But what about Ranger Mills? He'll have to meet you, Nate," I say.

The big guy nods. "His heart's in the right place. He's trying to save the park, and that means we're all on the same team, right?"

The sun is setting as the KTMC and Madison head through the forest toward Ranger Mills's office. As we get closer, we see him through the window, sitting at his desk with his head in his hands. We knock on his office door and wait until it finally swings open.

Ranger Mills looks down at us, and I can see the worry lines on his forehead. "Yes, campers? What can I do for you?"

"Actually," I say, "it's what we'd like to do for *you*. We found Bigfoot, and he'd like to meet you. No marshmallows needed."

"This isn't funny," Ranger Mills says. "I'm trying to save a park here. I don't have time for practical jokes."

He starts to close the door.

"It's not a trick!" Madison shouts, louder than I've ever heard her before. "We really *do* know Bigfoot, and he's trying to save the park, too. Come with us. Please."

We all stare at one another in silence until Ranger Mills steps outside, shutting the door. "All right. I'm trusting you."

The moon is rising in the night sky as we hike through the forest until we arrive at Nate's favorite log. Madison gives the call. The branches rustle, and when they part, Nate steps out in front of us. He has Earl, Frank, and Loretta with him.

Ranger Mills stares; his mouth hangs open, his

knees lock, and it looks like he's about to faint. "It's okay," Loretta says, "I did the same thing the first time I met him."

Nate steps forward and pats Ranger Mills on the head, just like he did Ava. "All better now."

We share our plan to save Peaceful Pine—a nature-based scavenger hunt with the prize being a fleeting glimpse of Nate.

"And along the way, people learn a lot about *all* the incredible life here," Nate adds.

For the first time during our whole visit, Ranger Mills smiles. "That's my favorite part of the plan," he says.

"Well, it's late, and I think our work here is done," I say. Ava, Sarah, Madison, and I stand up and start walking back to camp while Ranger Mills and his new friends continue talking.

Ava is practically skipping. "This was the best science field trip EVER!" she says, and Sarah and I look at each other. All we can do is laugh.

CHAPTER 11

IT'S ALL A BLUR

IT'S OUR LAST MORNING AT PEACEFUL PINE STATE Park, and we head straight for the back of the bus again. Sarah doesn't have to fight a pile of Puffy Pals this time, so Madison sits next to her.

"So, maybe Bigfoot *is* kind of special," Ava says, digging through her backpack for her camera.

Nobody says anything. We all stare at her with open mouths.

"What?" Ava says. "Not *all* Magicals. Only Bigfoot."

"O...kay..." Sarah says.

"You don't think so?" Ava asks.

"No...I mean, yes...Yes! I do think Bigfoot's special," Sarah says. "But the flying squirrels are great, too."

"Yes, of course the squirrels are great. I'm simply saying Bigfoot is special." Ava pulls her camera out of her backpack. "Not *all* Magicals. Just Bigfoot. You should give folks the benefit of the doubt, you know?

I'm a very open-minded person." Sarah raises her eyebrows at me, trying to hide her grin.

The bus ka-thumps along the gravel road, and I look up. Nate is standing at the top of Geezer Ledge. And he's not alone. Perched on his head and shoulders are Loretta, Earl, and Frank, who holds up a sign that says, DON'T FORGET TO SMELL THE ROSES. A new garden of bright red and yellow flowers surrounds them. They're all waving, and we wave back. No one else on the bus seems to notice.

"We need to figure out which pictures to use for *Creature Feature*," I say.

"I'm pulling them up now," Ava says. As she scrolls through the photos on her camera, the wrinkles on her forehead get deeper and deeper. "I don't understand what happened," she finally says.

"What?" I ask, looking over her shoulder as she scrolls.

"I can't believe this. Every photo," she says to herself. "Every. Single. One!"

Sarah and Madison lean across the aisle and we all look together. Every photo of Nate is nothing but a blur—a big, dark, furry blur. He could be a bear or ape or even a human walking through the woods. He's so blurry, you can't tell *what* he is exactly.

We all slump back against the bus seats. "How will anyone believe us?" Ava says.

"They'll have to take our word," I say.

"We can scan one of my sketches," Sarah says.

"Great idea! At least *we* know the truth." I pull my notebook out of my duffel bag as the bus rumbles down the road.

A long bus ride is a good a time to work on *Creature Feature*. I'm writing about our first encounter with Nate when I look at Ava next to me. Her eyes are closed, but I can tell she's not asleep. She's relaxed. Peaceful. So not Ava.

She leans over and takes a piece of paper out of her backpack. It's her signature stationery, the kind her grandmother gives her every year on her birthday. It's light blue with the atomic symbol at the top and her name—Ava Chen—underneath.

I sneak a peek out of the corner of my eye.

Dear Nate, it says. *I've been thinking. Marie Curie was an amazing woman. How would you feel about a trip to the 1890s?*

I smile to myself.

After three hours, the bus wheezes into our school parking lot. Yellow DO NOT CROSS tape is wrapped around all the playground equipment, including the benches where KTMC meets.

Mrs. Frisner stands at the front of the bus looking

at her phone. "According to Principal Howard, we have a Magical infestation…of some sort. We have to stay inside for recess…the *entire* week." A loud groan echoes throughout the bus, and Mrs. Frisner looks like she's about to cry. "We'll be spending every recess in our classroom. Together."

Ava looks across the aisle at Sarah, who looks over at me. Note to self—Magical infestation. Fairies? Gnomes? Goblins?

My mind is racing, but whatever Magical it is will have to wait until tomorrow. I have a blog post to finish.

Bigfoot, Peaceful Pine State Park